THE GUARD MOUSE

THE
GUARD

Story and Pictures by
DON FREEMAN

MOUSE

THE VIKING PRESS · NEW YORK

To
Tat and Bernice

Copyright © 1967 by Don Freeman
All rights reserved
First published in 1967 by The Viking Press, Inc.
625 Madison Avenue, New York, N. Y. 10022
Published simultaneously in Canada by
The Macmillan Company of Canada Limited
Library of Congress catalog card number: AC 67-10403

Pic Bk 1. Mice—Stories
2. London—Stories

4 5 6 7 8 80 79 78 77 76 75

SBN 670–35639–5

PRINTED IN THE U.S.A. BY REEHL LITHO CORP.

Just outside Buckingham Palace in the city of London there stands a guard named Clyde. It is his duty to keep small creatures from creeping through the openings along the Palace wall.

5

The Grenadier Guards treat Clyde with great respect. When they march past him they hold their heads erect and never blink an eye.

6

Clyde, too, always keeps his nose trained straight ahead and this, for a friendly mouse, is not an easy thing to do.

One foggy morning as he was about to go off duty, Clyde saw several creatures coming toward him in the haze. "Halt! Who goes there?" he challenged.

8

"It's me, Perry Petrini from New York City!" said a squeaky voice. "I've
brought my family to London to visit my cousin Clyde."

"Advance and be recognized!" commanded Clyde, none too certain that he
had heard correctly.

But when the Petrinis came into clear view Clyde forgot all about being a proper guard. He dropped his sword and ran to welcome his cousin Perry.

Then he greeted Madame Petrini and the three little Petrinis, Do, Re, and Mi.

"Jolly good!" he exclaimed, and took off his big black bearskin hat. "You couldn't have come at a better time. I'm free for a few hours and I can show you around London."

"We don't want to go anyplace," said Do. "We're tired."

12

"Can't we stay here, Uncle Clyde?" asked Re and Mi sleepily.

"Right-o," said Clyde. "You need a nap. My bearskin will do perfectly. You'll be quite safe and we'll be back a bit before eleven for the Changing of the Guard. You wouldn't want to miss that!"

Clyde tucked the youngsters snugly down inside his furry hat

and set it gently alongside his sentry box. Then he led Papa and Mama Petrini across Green Park toward Piccadilly.

"Press on!" he cried. "We'll just be able to catch that bus!"

The driver of the bus knew Clyde very well. He invited them to sit up front with him where they had a grand view of everything.

16

At Trafalgar Square the driver stopped the bus and his passengers got off.

"That's Lord Nelson up there," said Clyde proudly. "He won the Battle of Trafalgar."

18

But the Petrinis were more interested in what the pigeons were eating.
It reminded them that they hadn't yet had their breakfast.

19

"Of course, you're hungry!" said Clyde. "I know right where to take you next." They hopped into an empty vegetable barrow that happened to be passing and were carried directly to Convent Garden Market.

"This is where we Londoners get our food supplies," said Clyde. "Nobody will mind if we nibble a few tidbits."

Sure enough, in the early morning hustle and bustle the market men were too busy to notice them. Between nibbles Madame Petrini filled her beaded bag with fresh green peas for Do, Re, and Mi.

Clyde and his cousin feasted on grapes and carrot tips. When they had had plenty to eat Clyde said, "We've a lot to see so we had better step lively. Let's take to the roof tops."

"Are you going to show us London Bridge?" Madame Petrini asked hopefully.

"Rather!" said Clyde. "There's a high tower farther on that we can climb and from there we'll be able to see all the bridges along the Thames."

24

But Clyde had forgotten how slippery slates can be in the foggy weather. Suddenly he lost his footing and all three, hand in hand, went slithering down—

25

and landed kerplunk on the top of a gentleman's umbrella. "Good show!" said Clyde. "I say, umbrellas are safer than roofs."

26

Leaping from one umbrella to another, they traveled all the way down Whitehall to where Big Ben stands. "That's the most famous clock in the world," remarked Clyde. "It's a stiff climb up, but we can do it."

By the time they had scrambled up the side of the big stone tower the sun had burned away the fog. From their perch on the hour hand of Big Ben they had a perfect view of London and its great river Thames.

"Right below is Westminster Bridge," said Clyde, "and farther along, Waterloo, Blackfriars, and Southwark. And there's your London Bridge just this side of Tower Bridge."

28

At that very moment Big Ben began to strike the half hour. BONG! BONG!

"Hang on!" Clyde shouted. "There'll be six more bongs!"

cap. 4

Half past ten!

"Come along!" Clyde gasped. "We haven't a minute to lose! I have to be back for the Changing of the Guard."

Not since Hickory Dickory Dock has a mouse run down a clock so fast!

Once again they were in luck. A yellow sight-seeing bus was just leaving for Buckingham Palace. Clyde and the Petrinis dropped neatly onto the top of the bus, and rode away in style past Westminster Abbey

34

right to the Palace gates where a crowd was already gathering.

Clyde raced ahead to put on his bearskin.

But where was it? Where were the little ones he had left sleeping inside?

The Guards passed the word along: "Clyde's bearskin has gone missing!"

Soon the whole courtyard was in a royal dither! A Guard couldn't possibly go on duty without his bearskin hat!

40

The Queen leaned out her window to ask what all the excitement was about. A Guard explained and Her Majesty called in Scotland Yard.

But even the clever police were baffled. Here, there, and everywhere they searched until at last one of them shouted, "'ere it is!

And by Jove, there are three bloomin' mice inside!"

The little Petrinis were giggling. "A boy came by and thought Uncle Clyde's hat was a bird's nest!" said Do.

"Yes, and he thought we were three baby birds!" said Re.

"And he very kindly put us up in the tree!" said Mi.

44

The Guards all cheered: "Hip, hip, hooray!" Then the Sergeant Major roared out a command and they all fell into line, standing at rigid attention.

The band struck up a stirring march. The Changing of the Guard was finally under way.

And who do you suppose had the best view of all? The Petrinis, of course.
By special permission they sat on top of a royal lion's head

while Clyde stood proudly and happily at his post.